Trust Issues

AMY LAURENS

OTHER WORKS

SANCTUARY SERIES

Where Shadows Rise
Through Roads Between
When Worlds Collide
The Complete Sanctuary Series

KADITEOS SERIES

How Not To Acquire A Castle
How Not To Ring The Hero's Bell

STORM FOXES SERIES

A Fox Of Storms And Starlight

SHORTER WORKS

Darkness and Good
Dreaming Of Forests
Of Sea Foam and Blood
Trust Issues

NON-FICTION

How To Create Cultures
How To Create Life
How To Map
How To Theme
How To Write Dogs
The 32 Worst Mistakes People Make About Dogs

Find other works by the author at
http://www.amylaurens.com/books/

Trust Issues

AMY LAURENS

AUSTRALIA

Print ISBN: 978-1-925825-50-3
eBook ISBN: 9781393680352

www.inkprintpress.com

National Library of Australia Cataloguing-in-Publication Data
Laurens, Amy 1985—
Trust Issues
74 p.   cm.
ISBN: 978-1-925825-50-3
Inkprint Press, Canberra, Australia
1. Fiction—Fantasy—Urban 2. Fiction—Fantasy—Romantic

Summary: Becca goes on a date with werewolf Dane knowing it will be a disaster—and it is, but not for the reasons she expected.

First Edition: March 2020

Cover design © Inkprint Press.

TRUST ISSUES

Warm steam filled the air around Becca, faintly scented with fake apples from her shampoo. The hot water pattered down on her back, turning her skin red and, in theory, soothing away her tension. Of course, that would have been more easily facilitated had she not been in the midst of performing the contortions necessary to get her legs shaved, but she'd feel better once she was done. Probably.

Up, rinse, up, rinse; she scraped the blossom-pink razor over her pale legs, shaking it out in the main stream of the shower water at the top of each stroke. Steam billowed up in her face as she curled over her leg, warm against her cheeks and the inside of her nose.

There. Nearly done.

Honestly, the whole thing was an exercise in pointless futility. It wasn't like the wolf was going to be staring at her legs. And if he did, so what? Why did she care what he thought?

She didn't, that's what. Jaw clenching, Becca pressed shower water from her eye with the tips of her fingers.

One last stroke.

Becca inhaled sharply as the razor sliced the sensitive skin over her Achilles heel, removing a good slice of flesh and making the water run momentarily red. She grabbed at her ankle with her free hand, trying to stem the bleeding with her thumb, and nearly slipped on the wet tiles. Her elbow smacked the bottles of hair products that lined the shower's shelf—and the shelf itself—and she hopped madly, trying to regain her balance. Her weight fell against the cold glass of the shower screen—and the door screaked open, dumping her unceremoniously on the mat.

"Ow." That was going to bruise her butt.

Disgusted, Becca threw the razor back into the shower and scrambled to her feet. She reached in and turned the water off, realising as she did that her right elbow was about as tender as her butt would be in the morning. She flung her dark blonde, wet hair out of her eyes. So much for getting pretty.

Stupid date. Stupid wolf.

Red streaks on the mat caught her eye as she snagged her white towel off the rail: her heel, still dripping blood.

Bloody hell.

Literally.

She gathered her wet hair to one side, picking it off her shoulders and neck, wrapped the towel around herself, and hobbled to the vanity. Somewhere in there, lost amid cobwebbed piles of lotions, powders and unused potions, was a packet of bandaids.

Becca crouched awkwardly, stretching into the back of the cupboard that stank of bleach and toothpaste—and jumped as her sore elbow connected with something cold: a festering bottle of nail polish that was only too happy to jump off the shelf and smash on the floor, bleeding its awful browny-coral innards all over the second bath mat.

The chemical scent of the polish hit her nostrils. *Urgh. Someone remind me why I am doing this?*

Perching on the edge of the bath, Becca applied the bandaid, a giant strip wider than two of her fingers, its 'flesh' tones doing nothing to blend in with the complexion her grandmother had liked to call porcelain. "Bloody Irish," she muttered. She smoothed the plaster down, snatched up the bloodied bathmat and took it to the laundry, then stalked back to her room to dress.

Underwear, now that was a question. Not that there was any *question* of him *seeing* her underwear. She was widowed, not desperate. Even if, just occasionally, when he turned his big stupid wolf eyes on her she lost her mind just a little bit remembering what sex had been like.

But back to the underwear, she reminded herself as she finished towelling off and used the damp towel to twist up her hair. She didn't trust him as far as she could throw him, which given she doubted she could even lift him off the ground amounted practically to not at all—but could she really bring herself to go plain black cotton on a date?

Ah, screw it. It wasn't like the dress was that fitted or anything. Comfy it was. Becca fished her favourite pair of black undies out from the crumpled mess in her top drawer, donned a sensible—if slightly uplifting—bra, and from the very back of her other top drawer snatched out an old, dusty satin pencil case, the magenta one with the floral embroidery.

Despite nearly stabbing herself in the eye with mascara she hadn't applied in years, and overdoing it with the big round hairbrush and the hairdryer so it looked like she was wearing a 1960s wig for a few minutes until she managed to de-volumise things a bit, Becca managed to finish getting ready with a relative minimum of fuss.

She slipped into her little black dress—always go with a classic on the first date, she'd decided;

she still wasn't actually sure whether she wanted to impress the wolf or scare him away—slipped her phone, driver's licence and bank card into the cunningly placed pocket, straightened the short sleeves, and squished into a pair of heels that were dangerously tall and stunningly gorgeous: black satin with red and gold oriental designs brocaded into the fabric, nearly six inches high.

She wobbled for the first few steps before re-membering how to balance right in them: Weight on the toes, pretend the shoes aren't really there, just tip-toe along with your calves tight and your core strong.

You got this.

She caught sight of her reflection in her dresser mirror and sighed, confidence deflating. It had been so long since she'd done this. She'd been married to that two-faced jerk Nick for nearly three years, but they'd dated for another four or five before that.

She hadn't first-dated since she was what, eighteen? Nineteen?

Becca ran a hand over her forehead and exhaled. Nick was gone now. He might have stolen eight years of her life and literally any chance she ever had at having children of her own—the familiar flutter of regret and longing trembled through her stomach—but he was gone.

And the wolf was safe, at least inasmuch as he wouldn't lie to her upfront like Nick had.

Probably.

Maybe.

She hoped.

Really, there was no way to know. And trust wasn't exactly her specialty, when she was used to being able to detect lies and secrets right there in the head of anybody around her.

Urgh. Why, why am I doing this? This is such a bad idea.

As if on cue, her phone buzzed.

A message from her sister Clare: *I know he's picking you up in fifteen minutes, which means you're moping around wondering why you let me bully you into this, so I'm reminding you of our little bargain. Besides. He's gorgeous. It'll be good for you.*

Becca's lips quirked into a half smile. Her sister knew her all too well—hence the bargain, whereby Becca would be subjected to an endless stream of potential suitors every time she visited Clare if she didn't agree to a date with the wolf. And simply avoiding Clare's house wouldn't have worked; Clare would have just hauled the suitors to her.

A knock sounded at the door.

Adrenalin leapt through Becca's stomach and she bolted upright, stuffing her phone back into her pocket, then heading to the door.

"I'm sorry," Wolf-boy said as she opened it. "I know it's not fashionable to be early, but the traffic was better than I'd planned."

He'd left his longish hair down, a perfectly-styled tangle of honey-brown waves that screamed to be touched, and although he was wearing a dark suit, he'd left his baby-blue shirt open at the neck, and the combination did little to hide the sheer breadth and power of his shoulders.

His golden eyes drilled through her, soft and amused and completely, utterly focused on her.

Becca realised she was staring and closed her mouth, working the inside of her lower lip between her teeth.

So the wolf scrubbed up well. That changed nothing. She'd known since she'd met him that he was sex-on-legs. That, she'd learned the hard way, was not even *close* to the top ten most important things in a relationship. "It's okay," she said. "I'm ready."

She stepped out the door, forcing him to step aside for her, and locked up the house. "Ready?" The smile she gave him was too bright, brittle like it might crack any moment, and she tried to relax.

He studied her carefully for just an instant too long, but nodded. "Sure, let's go."

The drive to the restaurant was more silent than a morgue. *And I should know,* Becca added to herself, recalling the day she'd met the wolf-boy, when she'd been working a case as a consultant for her police buddy Karlie.

The silence didn't seem to bother him—*nothing* seemed to bother him—but by the time they pulled into the restaurant's carpark, Becca felt like electricity might start sparking from her fingers at any second.

With a sudden jolt of panic, she glanced down at her own chest, relieved to see nothing but her normal pale skin. Phew. Wouldn't do to have those come out tonight. The blood tattoos had been dormant since Nick had—since Nick had *died*, but knowing him they'd be keyed to activate at the worst possible time. She shuddered and pressed a hand to her belly, swallowing down the nausea that the memories still dredged up.

"You okay?" Wolf-boy's voice was quiet and matter-of-fact, like he knew exactly what she'd been thinking about.

Damn him, he probably did. She hated this whole inability-to-read-his-secrets thing. This wasn't how it was supposed to go. Secret breaking was supposed to make people more trustworthy for her, not less.

And yet Nick, the little voice in the back of her head told her.

Shut up, she told it fiercely.

So one person had figured out a way around her magical ability to read other people's secrets. Didn't mean anyone else knew that. Aloud, she added, "I'm fine."

The wolfiness in his expression increased a little.

"Stop it," Becca snapped. "I told you: I'm fine."

His lips twitched. "I can see that."

Lacking a sufficiently cutting reply, Becca flung the passenger door open, clambered out with only the smallest of inelegant wobbles, and slammed the door.

Wolf-boy rounded the car to meet her and offered her his arm.

Becca pointedly ignored it and stared up at the restaurant. "What even is this place?" Gaudy yellow and red signs declared it to be the Toro Gritando, cobwebs and cracked finishings declared it to be somewhat past its use-by date, and the noise and music streaming out of it declared it to be probably cheesy but definitely busy.

Becca sighed. Busy was a good sign, at least.

He shrugged placidly. "I like it."

Becca rolled her eyes. "Obviously, genius." She headed for the door, aiming for a stride but in reality ending up closer to a totter. Damn the six-inch heels. She should have known she was too out of practice.

"Hey." Wolf-boy caught up with her easily. "I know this wasn't exactly your first choice of Saturday night entertainment, but how about we at least try to keep this civil?"

She shot him a corner-of-the-eye look, and softened. After all, it wasn't his fault this was difficult. He'd been there to watch her back when no one else had; that didn't make it his fault that no one else had been there. "You're right." She gave a smile that wasn't all-the-way charming, but at least avoided brittle-and-false. "I'm sorry."

He bumped shoulders with her as they walked, an affectionate gesture between two equals. Sparks flittered down Becca's spine, and she couldn't tell if they were good or bad.

Really, it didn't matter, she thought as she clamped her teeth down on the inside of her lip to stop her eyes from filling up with tears. Stupid thing to get shaken up over. But it was the simplicity of the gesture that had disarmed her: no one had touched her in such a casual, intimate way for months, and she hadn't realised how much she'd missed it.

Deep breaths, she told herself as they climbed the steps. *You'll be fine.*

The scent of melting cheese and spicy chilis and flame-grilled beef threaded around them as they entered.

Wolf-boy—Becca sighed, and mentally corrected herself. *Fine. Dane.*

See? She could use his name without a problem. Dane conferred with the front of house waiter for a moment, then ushered her over to a table with a silvered 'Reserved' sign on it. The table sat nicely in the corner at the back of the room: perfect view over the restaurant, direct line of sight to the front door, close to the emergency exits and the bathrooms.

Impressed despite herself, Becca raised an eyebrow at him. "Did you pick the table, or did they?"

He took her one eyebrow and raised it to two. "What do you think?"

"Mm." Becca pursed her lips noncommittally and slid into the booth that backed the wall.

It probably would have made more sense to let Wolf-boy—*Dane*—have that seat, because she could sense trouble without needing line of sight, and although his powers were certainly interesting and incredibly useful, she was still pretty sure he couldn't spot trouble behind his back, but whatever. Tonight she needed all the security she could get.

A waiter appeared and flourished a red-and-yellow menu card that had seen better—cleaner—days at her, produced a bottle of tap water for the table, and disappeared.

"You think they get trained how to do that in waiter school?" Becca said idly, staring at the menu without reading it.

"What's that?"

"The whole appearing-disappearing genie thing they have going on."

"They only do that at good restaurants."

Becca's gaze flicked up to meet his, and she searched his face for any sign of the smugness she was sure ought to be there.

Nothing.

Instinctively she pressed with her secret breaking powers, but as ever she might as well have been trying to read a brick wall. And she still couldn't figure out why—why his shapeshifting abilities, and those of his friends, seemed to utterly block her ability to hear what was going on in the deep, secret places of their minds.

"You really can't read me, can you," he said, bemused.

"No." Becca snapped the menu up in front of her face. "Stop gloating." She glanced at him over the list of mains.

His light eyes laughed, but his voice remained solemn. "Nothing funny about it at all."

"Hmm." She pursed her lips and settled down to actually read about her dinner options. Which, she realised as she made it partway down, actually sounded really good. Damn him. Was perfect taste in food yet another star she'd have to add to his blindingly shiny and arrogantly polished crown?

"Look," he said, laying his own menu back on the table. "About what happened—"

Becca's stomach knotted as adrenalin flooded her system. "I don't want to talk about it."

"Becca," he said gently. "It's been seven months, and you've answered my calls what, twice? Maybe three times? Who else do you have to talk to about this? I know you're close to your family and all, but they weren't there, they don't understand what it was like…"

She opened her mouth for a cutting response, but something about him looked… haunted.

Maybe she wasn't the only one who'd suffered through months of bad dreams. She exhaled slowly. "Fine."

"Fine?" His whole body language changed, perking up like a… Dammit. She groaned. Like a bloody wolf scenting a bloody rabbit.

I am not a rabbit! She realised he was staring at her, and that her expression was not exactly friendly, and made a deliberate effort to soften it. *I'm still not a rabbit, though.* "Fine. You want to talk about it, get it off your chest, shoot. I'm listening."

That confused him. "I thought *you* might want to talk."

"All evidence indicates to the contrary, Wolf-boy." Oh, charming. Had she really just called him Wolf-boy to his face? Why yes, yes she had. So much for diplomacy.

The strangled expression on his face could have been smothered laughter, or choking rage. Either way, the chances of anything going right tonight were rapidly diminishing.

But luck, it seemed, was in her favour. Before he could draw himself together enough to reply, the waiter reappeared. Becca turned, the 'we're not quite ready could we have another few minutes' speech all prepared, and was caught with her mouth open as the waiter flourished a dome-covered silver tray at her.

"For the lady," the waiter pronounced, accent suspiciously thick, like he was laying it on deliberately. "A pre-dinner gift."

Heart pounding, Becca cleared space for the dinner-plate sized tray on the table automatically. The waiter disappeared again, and Becca stole a glance at her dinner partner's face. His expression made her stomach churn: eyes narrowed distrustfully, lips puckered.

Mouth dry, palms sweaty, Becca plucked off the white card that had been affixed to the silver dome.

For you. D.

Puzzled, she searched his face again. "Did you arrange this?"

His expression deepened to a frown, tension written in the lines of his shoulders. "No."

Becca sniffed—but on the other hand, at least he was being honest with her.

Maybe.

Probably.

Who the bloody hell knew? Not her, because he was a stupid *werewolf*, and her powers didn't work on him.

"Should I open it?" She let her fingertips run over the smooth curve of the dome's handle.

Warm. An entree, maybe?

Dane shrugged, a tiny, tight gesture. "Let me," he said, and reached.

Becca's fingers tightened reflexively around the handle. "I've got it," she said. She whipped the dome away—and froze, silver dome still in the air in her right hand, mouth open in a soft 'O'.

The creatures on the platter likewise froze momentarily: a knot of perhaps ten or fifteen short, sleek fish, about as long as her hand from fingertip to wrist, grey—and floating.

In the air. In a tight, three-dimensional cylinder.

In an instant, chaos reigned.

Dane grabbed her hand and tried to slam the dome back down over the fish, but they were too quick, streaking away from the platter—straight up into the air above the table, a smear of grey as they schooled upward.

The sharp 'ding' of the dome slamming down on the platter rang out—and the fish rearranged themselves into a line, facing down at Becca and Dane, teeth bared.

Ah, Becca realised as her pulse leapt at her throat. Not fish.

Sharks.

"What the hell?" Her voice was too high, didn't sound like hers.

"Don't. Move." Dane ground out, eyes fixed on the sharks.

Becca risked a quick glance at him.

Adrenalin jolted her: she hadn't seen him this tense since… Since they'd dispatched her former husband.

Swallowing hard, she stared back up at the sharks. "What are they?" she murmured, trying to keep her mouth from moving too much.

"Cookie cutters," he said, inexplicably.

But before Becca could demand an explanation, the sharks dove.

Dane flung the platter into place over her head and held it there as sharks bounced off with tinny, metallic thuds.

A nearby patron screamed.

"Dane."

He ignored her.

"Dane, the label was signed 'D'. Did you do this? Are those yours?"

The scent of something burning curled out from the kitchen.

"Come on," Dane muttered. "I need to get you out of here." He stood, snatched her by the wrist, and began dragging her toward the front of the restaurant.

In principle she wanted to protest.

In practice, she couldn't pry herself free of his grip for love or money or trying, and he was taking her in the direction she wanted to go anyway, which was *out*, so whatever. Fine. She'd take up the whole dragging thing with him later.

Another screamed rang out behind them, and suddenly every person in the restaurant was stampeding for the front door.

They'd been sitting up the back of the restaurant; at least a quarter of the guests hit the front doors at the same time, and in an instant formed a human road block.

Dane jerked her around by the wrist, changing course for the bar.

"Ow, hey!" Becca stumbled after him, nearly breaking an ankle as one of her absurdly high shoes wobbled.

She kicked them off as Dane glanced first back at her, then up in the air above her head.

Now barefoot on the cool beige tiles that surrounded the bar, Becca glanced up as well.

She flinched. The row of sharks had obviously been chasing her to the front door, and were now in mid-pivot as they streamed back toward her and dove.

Becca threw her free arm up over her head.

Dane jerked at her other arm. "Come on!"

She stumbled after him as he dragged her around the bar, through a thin cloud of acrid smoke that puffed out as a waiter dove for safety into the kitchen.

At the front door, patrons were shouting and occasionally screaming as they tried to mash themselves out as fast as humanly possible.

Dane paused for a moment behind the bar, the wall covered in brightly coloured bottles and glasses, the counter an old, dark wooden thing that looked like it might have once been a castle siege door, it was so massive.

Under it was a cutout area, big enough maybe for a dishwasher and a half, currently storing cardboard boxes full of—serviettes and card coasters bearing the restaurant's logo, Becca surmised as Dane set about quickly shifting them.

"In here," Dane said.

It was a dead end. A literal hole in the wall.

The sharks would pen them up there and take bites out of them one at a time.

"Come on!"

Dane crouched, tugging on her arm.

A shark snapped, neatly severing off some of Becca's hair. She swatted it away and folded herself over her legs, scrambling under the counter.

Dane shoved her against the back, covering as much of the opening as he could with his own body, snatching a couple of black plastic serving trays from the counter above to block the rest.

It stank of beer and a drain that desperately needed cleaning under the bar.

But on the up side, the sharks did seem to be reluctant to attack. From what Becca could see through the cracks between Dane's body and the trays, the sharks were hovering about two feet away, the whole school—was that what you called a group of sharks? It seemed far too tame—arrayed like darts, noses toward her and Dane's hidey hole, black-tipped, forked tails fanning out in every direction.

"Hold this one for a sec." Dane wriggled one of the serving trays. "Don't let your fingers show."

"What? How?" She grabbed the tray and tried to grip it so no fingers were showing outward, but it was impossible.

Meanwhile, Dane stretched up and out of their hiding spot, twisting lithely in a half crouch to hunt around on the counter above.

Becca heard the clink of glasses rattling together, and then a rushing clatter as cutlery spilled everywhere, including a couple of forks that bounced onto the floor.

Dane returned, swatted in front of the trays at a shark that was making a run for Becca's fingers, and retreated back into position.

"Here," he said, swapping something for the tray Becca was holding.

It was a knife, serrated, wooden-handled with three shiny, metallic circles where the handle was held together, the blade about as long as her hand.

"What's this for?" It was definitely better than nothing, but she didn't really see how it was going to help them fight the sharks off.

Although...

She squinted suspiciously at Dane in the shadows under the bar. His dark blond hair was tousled now, several strands caught in the stubble on his cheek, but the way he sat blocking her from the sharks, lounging on one hip with his legs twisted to the right, leaning against the wall to his left, two trays blocking the air above his legs...

He seemed more angry than afraid, which was fine, he was a shifter and he healed fast...

But also, the sharks weren't attacking him.

Becca poked him in the shoulder a little harder than strictly necessary. "What is going on?" she hissed, right as Dane glared at the sharks and said, "She's with me. Back off."

"They're sentient?"

"Semi," he said, still staring them down.

"Why aren't they attacking you?"

Dane ignored her, and Becca realised that the restaurant around them had gone quiet.

"Dane," she said. "Why aren't they attacking you?"

Scenes replayed in her mind: the sharks, released from their serving dome, immediately honing in on her; the sharks, following her through the crowd as she and Dane tried to run.

It made no sense. There was an entire restaurant full of people, and they didn't take the chance to snap a bite out of someone else?

Becca ground her teeth and shifted her weight, leg cramping from being stuffed under the counter, toes going cold on the tiles. The movement stirred up the drain smell. She wrinkled her nose.

"Dane. The sharks are targeting *me*. I think I have a right to know what's going on. What do you know about them?"

"Cut my arm," he said, eyes never leaving the sharks.

"What?" Her voice squeaked an octave higher than usual. "Your *arm?*"

"Yes, my arm." He sounded impatient, as though he was concentrating hard on something—and perhaps he was, she realised, seeing as how he still hadn't stopped staring at the swarm—pack—school—whatever—of flying, snapping doom out there.

"Wait," Becca said, giving her head a shake. "You're changing the subject. What do you know about the sharks, and why are they chasing *me?*"

"Becca," he said tightly. "I can't hold them off forever. I need you to trust me."

Trust him.

Again.

It was one thing following him into a hiding place that at least kind of logically made sense. But this? This was absurd.

She flashed back to the last time he'd asked her to trust him, right before he'd disappeared from view and left her to Nick.

That was when…

She swallowed hard, thighs squeezing together involuntarily.

It wasn't Dane's fault, and the deed had already been done, for the most part: Nick had already covered her, head to toe, in needle-fine carvings that wound and threaded together, whirling in individual patterns that connected together into a mind-bending whole.

Even if she'd been able to go with Dane right there and then, it wouldn't have changed much.

It would have changed what she knew, because as Dane had disappeared, Nick had returned to gloat—and it was only that that had given her the clue she'd needed to tug on to figure out how to submerge the tattoos that had come out in the pattern of the carved lines a day or two later.

But it wouldn't have changed what had happened.

She crossed her legs tighter, trying to suppress the other memories of what Nick had done, the reason she now knew she'd never be able to bear children again—and what he'd done to…

Becca pressed the back of her hand to her mouth, eyes scrunched closed as she forced herself to breathe through the memories.

He was dead.

He'd abused her in every possible way, he'd… He'd destroyed their unborn child.

But he was dead.

And Dane had come through. He'd gotten her out before Nick could activate the tattoos and turn her into a mindless automaton who existed only to serve his wishes, with her body—and her magic.

"You okay?"

Dane's voice snapped her back to reality like a knife.

"Fine," Becca said, irritated at how shaky her voice sounded.

Seven months. She'd had counselling. She'd been to therapy. She hadn't spiralled in a couple of months. She was fine. *Fine*.

"You started shivering," Dane said quietly, a quick glance at her out of the corner of his eye.

The concern in his expression gutted her.

"I'm fine."

"Mm hmm," he said noncommittally. "And your eyes are just leaking."

Becca swatted the tears away. "It's the smell," she snapped. "It reeks under here. You know I can't stand the smell of beer."

"Your first job," he said softly. "I remember."

Her stomach twisted again, but this time it was a little more fluttery. He remembered something she'd mentioned once, offhand, a quiet moment in the midst of a chaotic situation.

She wasn't sure how she felt about that.

"I can't hold them off forever," Dane said, and Becca realised his arms were trembling. Not consistently, not hard, but just a tremor now and then—which meant a normal human's muscles would be spasming right now.

"Fine." Becca clenched her jaw and the knife. "Where?"

"Bicep," said Dane. "It'll hurt less."

Becca blinked. "A, how deep are you expecting me to cut you, and b, you'd have to take your shirt and jacket off. Not that I'm protesting, but your hands are kind of busy right now." She tilted her head toward the black plastic trays.

His hands and arms *had* to be cramping by now.

As if he'd heard her thoughts, he growled under his breath, then said, "I can't shelter you here forever. Just cut the back of my hand."

She blinked at him again. "You're mad," she said. "I hope you know that."

"If I wasn't before, I am now."

Anger tightened in Becca's chest. Fine. She'd cut the stupid wolf, and she'd enjoy it. She readjusted her grip on the knife, steadied Dane's hand with her free hand, and sliced.

"Ow, *shit!*"

"You told me to cut you!"

Dane drew a long breath in, hissed it out through pursed lips, and cut her a sharp glance. "Now smear it on you."

"...the *frick*, Dane? *Smear* it on me? What are you, drunk?"

Becca jerked back; she'd gotten too close to the opening and a shark had tried to wriggle its way through the gap left between the rounded corner of the tray and the square corner of the bench.

Dane used the tray to smack it back to the others with a sharp, satisfying thud like a bat hitting a ball.

"Rebecca, you listen to me, and you listen real good. Yes. These sharks are after you. They're mine, and they're trained, and once they have your scent, they will not let you go."

Becca didn't know whether to lunge at him or punch him or what. Probably all of the above simultaneously. But before she could, Dane continued speaking.

"I didn't set them on you. I swear it." He cut her another glance. "You think if I wanted you hurt I'd do it like this? This is amateur hour, Rebecca, and there are way too many norms around."

True.

She didn't need her secret breaking senses to know that that's how Dane thought. If he wanted her dead, she would be, and she wouldn't even know about it until about five seconds after it happened.

A chill slid through her. Not a pleasant thought.

"I'm holding them off the best I can, but I can't do this forever. They have one impulse, and one only, and I'm fighting it, but eventually, they are going to win."

Now that she looked, he did seem a lot sweatier than he ought to be, given he was just holding up a couple of plastic trays while reclining against a wall.

"So what, I just… smear your blood all over me?"

He sniffed. "If only. That would be the easiest solution. Unfortunately, it would also take a lot more blood than I have to spare right now. Sorry."

Becca raised an eyebrow as he shot her a tight grin.

Joke? Maybe.

Still. She sighed explosively and snatched at his hand. She rubbed the back of her free hand over the cut she'd made, ignoring the way he tensed as she dragged over the cut that was, she realised, actually pretty deep.

Damn. Place kept sharp knives.

"There. Now what?"

"Pressure points," he said, and she realised his voice was getting rougher. "As many as you can."

Quickly, she dabbed the blood on her temples, on her forehead, nose and chin, a couple of places around her collar bones…

Gently, she squeezed the cut on Dane's hand to encourage more blood, then daubed that on the inside of her arms, the backs of her knees, and a few places around her ankles and feet.

There were a couple more key pressure points she could think of off the top of her head, but none she could reach without taking her dress off—or at least, none she could *decently* reach without taking her dress off—and *that* was not going to happen.

"Enough?"

Dane pursed his lips. A tremor ran through his arms, the trays flapping.

Tentatively, Becca grabbed the closest one, breath held as she wrapped her fingers around the edges of it.

It was only when nothing happened that she realised she'd been hunched up, bracing for an attack. She let out a long breath and forced her shoulders to relax.

"I think… I think we can lower the trays now," Dane said, voice heavy with exhaustion. He let his drop.

Becca was a little slower to follow suit—but when the sharks failed to take advantage of the opening Dane's lowered tray made, she cautiously let hers fall as well.

Eleven sharks, now that she could count them properly, all arrayed in a partial dome around the hole under the counter, fins wafting gently, gills pulsing in and out. Her breath hitched as one bared its pointed teeth—but a growl from Dane kept it where it was.

Becca softened against the side of the hidey hole, head tilting against the cool laminex as though it had suddenly become three times too heavy. She shifted, flexing her feet in an attempt to ease the pain in her left ankle and right calf.

Dane exhaled audibly. "Okay. I think that's—"

He was cut off by a shark darting suddenly toward Becca, aiming at her now-exposed ankle.

Dane hit it sharply with the tray he was still holding.

There was the thud as the tray connected with the shark—and a smash, as a glass teetered over the edge of the counter and shattered on the floor, a cloud of yeasty beer-smell enveloping the bar.

"Ow," Dane said, grimacing and rubbing his head where he'd hit the underside of the counter.

Becca's heartbeat raced, her breathing shallow and too fast, and the stink of beer was suddenly too much, and her stomach began to writhe.

Dane frowned, and resumed the intense stare at the sharks that he'd been maintaining before. A bead of sweat rolled down his temple. "Are you bleeding?"

"What?" Becca swallowed and clenched her fists, willing her stomach to stay put. Even the drain smell had been better than this. At least no one had ever assaulted her while she'd been cleaning a drain.

"Are you bleeding?" Dane glanced at the band-aid, now visible on her ankle. "Something's drawing them to you still. Blood. Is there blood anywhere?"

Becca's fists clenched tighter. "I'm covered in blood, you freak!"

Another shark darted in, right toward her ankle. Dane popped it on the head, and it struggled helplessly on the floor for a moment until it got its fins under it again.

"I meant *your* blood," he ground out. "Obviously."

Becca snorted. "Not obviously." The nausea was getting stronger. Any second now, Dane wouldn't need to play whack-a-shark, because she'd drench them in the contents of her stomach.

Still. They'd probably like that.

Oh, ew. Becca winced at the mental image of the sharks chowing down on vomit, probably turning on each other in the process since they'd all be covered in it.

"Rebecca," Dane said through gritted teeth. "This is not a great time for an argument. Are. You. Bleeding?"

"My ankle." Becca twisted her foot around so Dane could see the bandaid more clearly. "I cut it shaving."

Dane muttered something under his breath.

"Pardon?"

"Nothing. Give me your ankle."

Becca rolled her eyes. "Oh, sure, because I'm contortionist in my spare time."

Dane swivelled abruptly around to pin her in his gaze. "Rebecca Capello—"

"Klar," Becca interrupted.

Dane stared.

"I'm using my maiden name again."

Dane blinked, shook his head, and swore. "Rebecca Klar, I have known people who would literally die rather than face these sharks. If you don't want to be one of them, give me your ankle."

She lifted her foot and let it drop none-too-delicately in his lap. "That doesn't make sense, by the way. Telling me I don't want to be someone who'd rather die than face the sharks. It's almost entirely meaningless as a threat."

She winced as he ripped the bandaid off, jaw tight and eyes narrow as his gaze flicked between her ankle and the sharks.

Another bead of sweat rolled down his temple.

"Where's the knife?"

Her heart leapt. "Why, are you going to amputate my foot? Because that would just create more blood, you know, although I suppose you could chuck them the foot to keep them busy while we run, except of course I won't be running because of aforementioned amputated foot, though I guess you could carry me.”

Dane ignored her babbling, since she’d done as he’d asked and passed him the knife anyway. He glanced down at the cut she’d made across the back of his right hand, then picked at it with the knife so it started bleeding again. “Sorry about this,” he said, and it was the grimness in his eyes that scared Becca most.

No, nonono, he’s actually *going to cut my foot off…*

He gripped her ankle tightly and used the knife to scrape the scab away from her shaving wound.

Becca hissed inward, but kept her leg still. After all, at least she still had her foot.

He’d protected her before. He’d fought on her side. He wasn’t Nick.

But then he pressed the bleeding back of his hand against the now-bleeding scrape on her ankle, and fire shot through her body, rolling up from her feet and exiting with a tingle in her scalp, and for one, breathless, airless second it felt like the incisions Nick had carved in her body, the ones intended to enslave her to his will, to let him control her secret breaking magic entirely—and Becca screamed.

Faint marks shone everywhere her bare skin could be seen, precision-thin lines glowing white like scars, or UV tattoos.

He'd activated her carvings, the marks that Nick had given her.

Weeks, it had taken her, to figure out how to hide them under her skin, and now he'd brought them back again, and there they were, right before her eyes, the proof that the man she'd called her husband, the man she'd trusted with her life, had abused *everything* about their relationship to subdue her, had taken her trust and shattered it beyond repair, and she was breathing too fast, too shallowly, she couldn't get enough oxygen and things were going blurry…

"Go on now," Dane said sternly, and at his voice, Becca's vision began to clear. "Go home."

The sharks hesitated for half a second, then turned as one and swam purposefully off.

Becca watched them go, still breathing hard. They rose effortlessly to clear the counter, then swam off through the air in the direction of the front door.

For a second, she wondered how they'd get out—but there was a gentle thump, and then the tinkling of the bell over the front door.

"Lucky it's a push," she murmured, because what else could she say that wasn't equally absurd right now?

And the alternative at this point was hyperventilating, and she was trying hard not to do that, so hard, oh gosh, her pulse was going to shatter her eardrums, and her stomach was heaving…

Dane touched her cautiously on her knee.

His fingers were warm.

Something zinged between their skin, and the tattoos there glowed brighter, while everywhere else on her body, they dimmed.

"You okay?"

Becca swallowed hard. "Sure," she said, voice hoarse, scratchy.

The back of her neck itched, a familiar buzz that her secret breaking senses made whenever someone around her was telling a lie, or trying to keep something specific a secret.

Becca slapped at her neck and whipped around.

"Dane, there!" She pointed to the kitchen, where a stubbled man in chef's attire was peering at them through a narrow crack in the door.

Dane leapt to his feet, scrambling over her.

The man rabbited.

Dane barged into the kitchen with a well-placed shoulder against the door, not even slowing down.

"Lucky it's a push," Becca murmured again. All the stress and anxiety bubbled up inside, and she broke into giggles so hard she snorted—then sighed, hands pressing over her still flip-flopping stomach.

She sighed again.

"Right," she muttered. "Around the back."

Becca stood, a little light-headed, and ran for the front door. It slammed behind her as she pivoted right and ran for the alley that led around to the restaurant's trade entrance, hoping beyond hope that it was a dead end and their rabbiting chef would have no other way to avoid her.

He didn't. Coming toward her at a dead run was their rabbit, and Becca braced herself, heart hammering, toes flexing against the cold concrete of the path. Those self-defence lessons she'd been taking since Nick were about to pay off.

Wait for it, Becca told herself. *Wait for it…*

The man was twelve metres away, ten, eight…

Pain lit over Becca's body, her tattoos firing into full, rich colour.

She screamed, and fell to her knees.

The concrete scraped against them, but it was nothing to the sudden, breath-taking pain of the tattoos lighting up all at once like a bonfire.

In front of her, the man froze too before dropping to the ground and curling up in a ball. "No!" he shouted. "No, make it stop!"

The air felt thick with fear, the stink of garbage from the alley overlaid with something metallic and bitter.

It hurt her ribs to breathe, and Becca fought to stay upright on her knees.

Ahead, further down the alley, Dane still made his way toward them, but he'd slowed as though trying to run through water instead of air.

What's going on? What's happening?

Darkness deepened in the already dark night until it felt like a physical weight, crushing her chest, weighing her shoulders down.

The tattoos prickled all over her skin, needle-points of pain and general sensation.

The chef groaned.

Becca swallowed, wetting her suddenly dry throat. She steadied herself with hands on the rough concrete, and pushed up to stand.

Her head spun, darkness clouding about the corners of her eyes.

Pressure intensified in her head.

Any second now her heart was going to pulse right out of her chest, and the nausea—which had dimmed, she hadn't realised with everything else going on—returned in full force.

She gagged.

Dane was nearly there, a handful of steps away.

Becca forced herself to move toward the chef, still lying curled up on the ground, now sobbing, though the noise seemed muffled, like Becca was hearing it through a thick layer of blankets.

She gagged again and stumbled.

Dane hurled the chef up by the scruff of his

collar, the man still trying to curl into a fetal ball, hands clamped around Dane's wrist. "I've got him," Dane said, glancing at Becca. "You can let go now."

Let go? Let go of what? The fecking, no-good, useless wolf—

Her thoughts cut off abruptly as the world whirled around her.

Dane had vanished.

So dark. Why was it so dark? She couldn't even see the stars.

Becca groaned and wrapped her arms around her stomach, doubling over as though it might help hold her stomach in.

The tattoos on her arms and legs glowed faintly in the night, a pale blue phosphorescence, eerie. She couldn't seem to convince her brain the tattoos were where her limbs were. They seemed disconnected from her, somehow, floaty.

They still stung, though.

And then Dane was back, pulling her upright gently but firmly, untangling her arms from around her stomach and threading his own arm around her for support. "There you go," he said soothingly, and Becca heard it as though from a distance. "I've got you. Just let go now, it's alright."

Let go of what?

She still had no idea what he was talking about.

"The tattoos," he said. "The magic."

She realised she'd voiced her thoughts aloud. "Oh."

Let go of the magic? What mag—

But as soon as she formed the thought, she realised she knew what Dane meant. The blue glow? It wasn't real. At least, she wasn't seeing it with her eyes, anyway.

Forcing her shoulders to relax, she breathed a long, slow breath out through pursed lips—and the glow faded away.

Immediately, the night brightened. Small insect noises returned—crickets chirping, something that was maybe a frog—and so did the stars.

The pain dimmed to a localised throbbing in her left big toe—she must have stubbed it on the concrete.

Becca tilted her head back against Dane's arm and stared at the fire-bright constellations above. The noise of the evacuated restaurant crowd filtered through into her consciousness, the rising and falling murmurs of quiet conversation. The night air breathed into the alley on a breeze, cool and fresh, like grass and clean stones and—yeah, nope, okay, there was the garbage again. She wrinkled her nose as the wind stilled and the stink of the skip bins clouded around her.

"I'm good," she said. "I'm good." The second time actually sounded like she meant it, too.

"I'll take you home." Dane led her toward the mouth of the alley and the murmuring crowd—and with every step, Becca's momentary calmness fled.

"What did you do with him?"

The line of Dane's jaw tightened. "I took care of him."

"He was the one who released the sharks, then?"

"Yes."

"Why?"

"Doesn't matter."

Becca's stomach flip-flopped. It wasn't just that her secret breaking senses made people actually *keeping* secrets from her equal parts irritating and stressful and disorienting.

It was also that the only people who could usually manage it were people who…

Who knew her well. Who knew how she operated—and how her talents operated.

Dane wasn't close to her.

And he knew her far too well.

She swallowed, mouth suddenly dry.

'Took care of him.' There was an obvious meaning there, of course, but what about the others? The other possibilities that *didn't* include

Dane punishing the guy for his actions in some way, because the guy had done what he was supposed to do?

Dane had admitted the sharks were his, hadn't he? When they were hiding under the bar?

He'd covered in her blood—which, now she came to think of it, seemed to have been burned away by the magic—he'd *cut* her and mingled his blood with hers, which, ew, she could only hope he didn't have anything contagious…

And something in her had changed.

His blood might not have had any normal human contagions, but the tattoos sure as heck had reacted to it. She'd felt that tingle wash over her, and then the tattoos had appeared, and they'd reacted to his touch, and then she'd gone all floaty.

Had he known that would happen?

She glanced up at him as they neared the mouth of the alley. "Dane, why did you rub your blood into mine?"

His jaw twitched, and—was it just a coincidence, the way they'd been stepping, or had his arm tightened around her fractionally for an instant there?

"Dane, did you know what would happen when you did it?"

"Just come to the car, Becca. No one else here needs to hear this."

He did tighten his arm around her this time, possessively, and he was glancing around the carpark as though looking for danger.

Well, Becca had had just about enough danger for one night, thanks very much. He could take his sharks and stick them down his pants.

"You knew, didn't you," she said, voice flat as she ran back over the night in her mind, even as her stomach was knotting in anger. "You knew something would happen."

If he wasn't a wolf, she might consider punching him.

"Not exactly."

They were nearly at the car. She still had her phone, though, didn't she? Becca shifted her hip, glanced down…

Yes, phone was still in place. Kudos to whomever had designed this dress, because it was a bloody miracle.

Anyway, she had her phone and presumably her bank card. She could call for a ride.

And his grip around her shoulders was too tight.

Becca stopped point blank, ducking a little so his arm skimmed over her. He nearly stumbled— nearly, not actually, because he was a shifter and they were bloody ninjas on their feet—and pivoted back to her, brows tight, chin jutting and clenched.

Becca tossed her hair and planted her hands on her hips. "What. The. Hell? I am *not* going home with you, but you're not going home either until you give me some answers. What did you do to me, Dane? *What did you do?*"

He strode away a couple of steps and stopped, body angled away from her, holding the back of his neck with one hand.

Something chill congealed in Becca's chest. A tiny part of her had still been hoping it'd been an accident. "What did you do?" she whispered.

He darted a glance at her and exhaled heavily. "I'm sorry."

Becca took a step toward him, sweating hands fisting at her sides. "Dane, you're scaring me."

"Good," he muttered.

"What. Did. You. Do?" She stared right into his yellow-brown eyes, daring him to ignore her.

For a moment he simply stared back, eyes flickering slightly as he searched her gaze—left eye, right eye, left eye, right. Then he sighed heavily and gave a quick little double-tug on his hair. "I was going to tell you about it tonight. The Pack have been researching your... You know."

"My present from Nick," she ground out.

He nodded. "Yes. A week ago, Aania found a reference to a source text that's held at the National Archives down in Canberra."

Becca tossed her hair back anew and folded her arms, right toes drumming on the pavement. "And let me guess, she and Carl took a road trip, and about two days ago they found something important, and when they let you know, you rang me and asked me out to dinner." She tilted her head. "Stop me if I'm missing something here."

He sniffed. "I mean, you glossed over the whole part about someone not wanting them to get the information, and the attack, and the fact that they got back yesterday pretty bruised and banged up, but yeah, something like that."

Becca forgot for a second that she was mad at Dane and let her mouth drop slightly open. "Someone attacked them?"

Dane softened. "They're shifters, Bec, they're okay."

She shook her head, fingers tightening around her upper arms. "I'm sorry." Seven months it had been since the big battle with Nick, where three shifters had died to keep her free; she thought she'd moved past the stage of her life where other people got hurt for her sake.

Her jaw twitched rapidly.

"Hey, Bec, it's okay," Dane soothed, taking a half step closer.

She tensed and angled her shoulder slightly toward him. "Tell me what they found."

"A variety of ways to activate your... marks. And some vague hints about what you might be able to do with them."

Becca blinked, her head snapping up to meet his eye. "Do with them?" Her pulse skittered.

Do with them? But they were supposed to be a punishment, a way of controlling *her*... They were something done *to* her, not... not something she could *use*.

She glanced back at the entrance to the alleyway and pursed her lips inwards, rubbing them together. The dark shadows, the stink of fear... She looked back up at Dane, questions widening her gaze.

He nodded, stepped forward, and enveloped her in a tight hug.

This time, she didn't protest.

"The sharks are mine," he murmured against her hair. "I confiscated them off an old sorcerer a couple years back. I... They were trainable," he continued, hands warm and sure, one on her shoulder, one on the bare skin of her upper arm. "But once they key into someone's scent, they're almost impossible to deflect. They won't go for me though, hence—"

"Smearing me with your blood," Becca said into his shoulder, nodding slightly. This close, she could smell the sweat she'd seen earlier.

He'd tried his best to protect her.

He *had* protected her. The only reason she'd been hurt was because she'd tried to help him take down the chef.

Well, that and he'd reopened her scab, but she'd been the one to actually *make* that wound.

How many times had Nick protected her, to make sure she was safe until he was ready to make his move?

She could think in circles like this for—

"Yes." His arms tightened around her for just a second, cutting through the spiral of her thoughts, then he exhaled loudly. "Usually, that should have been enough, but they could still smell your blood because of your open wound. I had… I had to, uh, mix our bloods to throw them off the scent."

The last part ran together a little, like he was glossing over something—but her secret breaker senses didn't work on shifters. She could argue, press the point… Or she could choose to trust him.

Her fingers curled around his lapel and she drew in a long, steadying breath.

He'd protected her.

How did normal people live like this?

Between rises in the crowd's conversations, she could hear his heart beating beneath his suit coat.

She swallowed, tasting remnants of the bitter smell from the alley. "That guy. In the chef outfit. Was he trying to kill me?"

Dane shifted his weight, his shoes scuffing slightly against the pavement. Probably surprised she hadn't pressed him about the blood thing. Becca smirked, just a little. So she could still surprise him too. That was a good thing.

"Yes."

"Does he know who I am? What I can do?" Her breath caught.

Another hesitation. "Probably."

She let out the breath. "And the tattoos?"

"Introducing my blood to your system activated them, like an immune response to an invader. I thought it might, given what Carl and Aania had found. I just had to hope my blood would last long enough to discourage the sharks."

Becca glanced at her hands. The tattoos were fading now, a mid-toned blue-grey colour in the yellow light streaming out from the front of the restaurant, rather than the deep black they'd been. "And the... the fear? In the alleyway?"

He nodded. "What Aania found wasn't super specific about what you might be able to do with the tattoos, but influencing the emotions of the people around you was a definite possibility."

"Oh."

Around them, people had obviously decided the restaurant wasn't going to reopen for the night. Most of them were getting into cars and leaving, the sounds of engines and doors closing like soft percussion in the night.

By the steps to the front door, a man argued over-loudly with one of the head waiters. Probably demanding his money back, or a free dinner as compensation or something.

A light breeze brushed over her face, bringing the scent of spices and grilled beef.

Becca swallowed, and this time there was no bitter, metallic gall of fear—just the lingering taste of her toothpaste in the corners of her mouth.

The man was still standing there on the steps, a gesticulating shadow against the bright light of the restaurant's front windows.

"Becca?" Dane said gently, and she realised she'd been staring at the arguing man vacantly. "Can I take you home now? Please?"

Becca sighed deeply and pushed away from him—not hard, just so she could balance upright without leaning against his warm chest. "My shoes are still in there," she said, tilting her head at the restaurant.

"Is that a yes?"

Out of the corner of her eye, she could see Dane searching her face. She shrugged. "It's not a no."

He exhaled as though in relief. "Go wait in the car," he said, handing her the keys. "I'll get your shoes."

Numbly, her hand closed around the keys, a point of cold in the comfortable night. "Okay," she said softly as halfway across the car park Dane climbed the steps to the restaurant, ignoring the protests of the wait staff, and let himself back in to Toro Gritando. "Okay."

She wasn't exactly sure *what* was okay—the soles of her feet were going to be screaming at her tomorrow, protesting her run on the concrete; she'd probably ache all over from using the tattoos.

Her knees were scraped, her hip was reminding her of the fall she'd had earlier, she was hungry, someone had probably just tried to kill her in a highly visible and messy way—which, she really needed to pick over that later...

But the key word there was 'later'.

Right now, Dane was collecting her shoes, and there he was, coming back over to her with a little smile on his face—"These ones?"—and even though the date had been an unqualified disaster, well, she thought as she accepted the shoes and, using him for balance, slipped the right one on, at least it had been someone *else* who had ruined the night, not either of them.

"Oh, and Becca?"

She glanced up at him, off balance and hanging off his sleeve as she held her left shoe with her foot half in. "What?"

Was she imagining it, or was he... blushing? She squinted at him, but it was hard to tell in the light. Hurriedly, she finished putting her shoe back on and stood, now nearly on eye level with him. "What is it, Dane?"

His gaze darted over her, and back into the distance. He swallowed. "I, um..."

She narrowed her eyes and put her hands back on her hips.

He sighed. "I think giving you some of my blood might have... changed things."

Becca rolled her eyes. "Well, duh. You saw what happen—"

"No." He twisted slightly so he was facing her exactly front on, something strange and... desperate, maybe? in his eyes. "No, I mean, something between us."

Becca frowned.

"Becca," he said slowly. "You know how you can't get a read off shifters with your secret breaking, how we talked about that being what life is like for everyone else?"

"Yes," she said slowly. Where on earth was he going with this?"

He swallowed again.

If his sudden attack of nerves didn't kill him, Becca would, because it was almost not possible to make this more awkward and suspenseful, and after the night they'd just had, she didn't appreciate it.

"I um, I kind of know what you mean now."

Becca frowned, brows knitting together.

Dane swallowed, more off kilter than she could ever remember seeing him before. "I can… I can hear your feelings," he said, voice husky.

Becca's eyes widened. "You mean…?"

He nodded, a bare, slight movement in the night. "If I'm standing close to you…" he said, looking down as he reached for her hand.

Becca let him twine his fingers in hers, her heart suddenly racing.

"…I can, well…" He met her gaze, and she remembered the first time she'd locked eyes with him like this, his golden brown irises drawing her in, his expression promising her everything she'd ever wanted and more. "I can feel what you're feeling," he murmured, gaze flicking between her eyes.

Her breath had gotten stuck in her throat somewhere. What she *was* feeling?

What was she *feeling*?

His fingers were laced in hers and he was staring at her like she was the most important thing in all the world—and her stomach gurgled.

Dane smiled, and let her go. "Come on," he said, and turned for the car. "We'll get some food on the way home."

Becca stood staring for a moment, watching the movement in the breadth of his shoulders as he made his way to the car, just a wolf heading for his property like nothing in the universe could stop him.

Becca shook her head, and snorted.

Well. It looked like she'd *have* to trust him now. That, or avoid him for the rest of their natural lives.

But somehow, she thought as she gave her head a shake and followed him to the car, avoiding him didn't seem likely.

And maybe—just maybe, no commitments now—that didn't have to be a bad thing after all.

ABOUT THE AUTHOR

AMY LAURENS is an award-winning Australian author of fantasy and science fiction for both adults and young adults.

She has written the award-winning portal-fantasy *Sanctuary* series about Edge, a 13-year-old girl forced to move to a small country town because of witness protection (the first book is *Where Shadows Rise*), the humorous fantasy *Kaditeos* series, following newly-graduated Evil Overlord Mercury as she attempts to acquire a castle, the young adult *Storm Foxes* series about love and magic and mental health, and a whole host of non-fiction, usually about dogs and writing.

You can find out more at
www.amylaurens.com.

Read more by Amy Laurens!

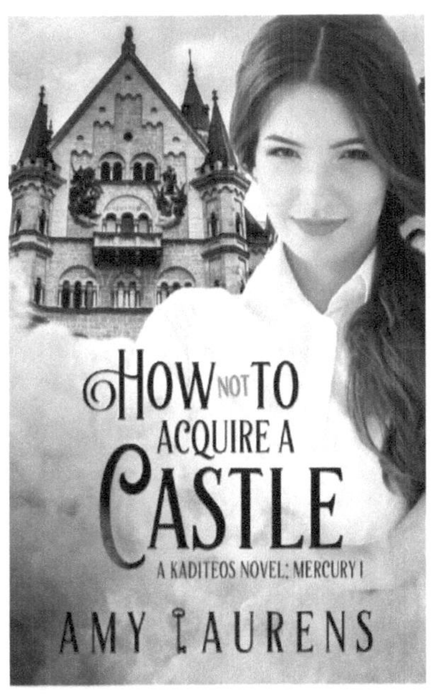

HOW NOT TO ACQUIRE A CASTLE

CHAPTER ONE

ON A HARD PLASTIC CHAIR IN THE FRONT ROW OF THE Great Hall in the world's fifth-best Evil Overlording Academy, with its red-wooden parquetry floor that spoke of wealth and the beige, square panels of sound-boards speaking of conservatism on the walls, Mercury sat, pointedly not sweating.

Partly, this was because the Academy Administrators had deigned to turn on the air-conditioning earlier in the day, in recognition of the fact that the hall would be packed out with approximately six hundred bodies, all here to celebrate the graduation of about a third of that crowd.

But mostly, Mercury was pointedly not sweating because she made it a point never to sweat, sweat being an indication that she was working hard, and hard work being antithetical to her way of life.

However. If she *had* been sweating right now, it would not have been due to the uncomfortable warmth of six hundred packed bodies that even the air-conditioning system couldn't completely shift, or, in fact, from over-exertion. Instead, it would have been caused by an even more unfamiliar concept in Mercury's emotional vocabulary: nervousness.

Mercury did not *get* nervous. Mercury got things *done*.

So the fact that she was sitting here, in the front row of the Great Hall, about to graduate from Evil Overlording Academy (with distinction), and was feeling *nervous*… She crumpled the black paper program in her pale fists. It made her furious, that's what it did. Abjectly furious, that snooty-tooty Deviran with his stupid morals and his stupid I-don't-want-to-be-here and his stupid Overlords-are-empty-figureheads and his stupid face sitting ten people over, looking implacable with his deep brown skin and barely-there, precision-groomed beard, as though he knew it gave him a stupid air of alluringly stupid mystery…

Mercury scowled and searched for the train of thought that had been derailed, yet again, by Deviran's stupidity.

Ah. Yes. She was angry because she was nervous because she wasn't absolutely entirely one hundred and fifty percent sure that she'd beaten Deviran in their final exams, and 1) being anything less than a hundred and fifty percent certain of anything made her cranky, and 2) being beaten by Deviran for dux of the year would be utterly unbearable. She flicked away a piece of fluff that had become snagged under her immaculately magenta-painted nails and smoothed out the black paper program.

In the front corner of the hall, the starkly-attired string quartet with their traditional black instruments began playing the March of the Oncoming Doom. The screechy scrapes of hundreds of chairs on the hall's wooden floor sounded as the crowd climbed to its collective feet.

Mercury sat with her arms firmly folded for a few moments longer, until her best friend Sparky kicked her in the ankle.

"Get up, idiot," Sparky hissed, hints of real flame flickering through her flame-coloured pixie cut.

"No," Mercury said, flouncing to her feet and tossing her own glossy brown hair back over her shoulders. Four years she'd been playing by the Academy's rules in order to get what she wanted, and she'd had just about enough. Other people's rules should only be applied to plebs too stupid to invent their own.

Sparky rolled her eyes somewhere over Mercury's head before focusing on the stage, where the ceremonial party had begun entering.

Mercury clenched her jaw and narrowed her own eyes as the teachers of the Evil Overlording Academy filed onto the stage, dressed in their formal finery. Each teacher had their own distinctive look that matched their personality and their Overlording style, from severe charcoal suits to jet-black leathers, pastel ballgowns and gem-toned lingerie and eye-blinding spandex, and even on one tiny old woman at the back, worn jeans and a grey flannel shirt. She was the one to watch out for, of course; Mercury could respect an Overlord who was confident enough in their abilities that they didn't need to telegraph them. It wasn't a look *she* would consider, of course, but still. She could respect it.

The band's march finished and, after a moderately awkward pause, the crowd sat. The Principal, pale skin and dark hair matching his suspiciously vampiric red-and-black suit, took the podium, and Mercury narrowed her eyes. He was doing a superb job of hiding his emotions—he was a premier Evil Overlord, after all—but she was Mercury, and unlike anyone else, she had the benefit of being able to rummage through people's consciousnesses. She was better at adding things *into* people's minds than taking information out, but he was telegraphing fear loudly enough that she could sense it without trying overly much.

Mercury pursed her lips. Hmm.

The Principal cleared his throat at the blackened-wood podium, and the fear made it into his usually-unreadable eyes. "Before we begin," he said, and Mercury's stomach did a peculiar kind of flip-flop. "I have a pressing announcement to make regarding the safety of our students and their families." He cleared his throat again and took out a sheet of paper from his pocket, unfolding it carefully and smoothing out the creases before beginning again. "The Council"—quiet booing echoed around the hall, and Mercury tsked impatiently—"have asked me to recommend that students from Tumul Tuos seriously consider postponing their return to town for a few days. The city is dealing with a *situation* at present which may present a danger to our students' health and safety."

Mercury's hands fisted at her sides and she forced herself to remain seated. What was wrong with her city? What had the Council mucked up now? A risk to the students' safety? There had to be more he wasn't telling them. Gently, Mercury tugged on his consciousness, implanting the suggestion that it might be better to share the news than to keep it secret. After all, how could they fight an enemy they didn't know?

"There are, ah…" He trailed off, glancing side to side as though wondering why his mouth had decided to continue.

Mercury didn't snicker, but she did press her lips together in satisfaction.

The Principal took a deep, steadying breath and seemed to change tack. "There has been one death already. The family have already been notified, so it is with much regret that I must inform you that Woovermyer will no longer be with us at the Evil Overlording Academy."

Murmurs broke out around the room, not all of them sad—to be expected in a school devoted to raising the next generation of dictators (ish) and despots (of sorts).

Mercury, however, crushed her program in her left hand, fist so tight her nails bit her palm.

"You okay?" Sparky murmured, leaning toward her.

Mercury gave a single, tense shake of her head and stared at the podium. Dead. Livie Woovermyer was dead in *her city*. And the Council hadn't done anything to stop it. Couldn't do anything to stop it, probably, given they'd warned the students to stay away. Livie hadn't been the strongest candidate in the year level, but she was no lightweight, either. It would take a lot of power to kill a Seven.

Enough was enough.

A good thing Mercury was about to graduate at the top of the class, giving her the right to knock the lowest ranking current Overord off their perch. Tumul Tuos would be hers in a matter of hours. And then there'd be no more of these wasteful deaths. Her city would be safe at last.

Madame Pompadour was up the front now, elbow gloves the same glimmery silver colour as her elaborate, piled-curls wig, eyelids gleaming with matching silver eye shadow, and abruptly Mercury realised Madame was there to make the announcement that would change her life forever.

She leaned forward in her seat, ready to stand when her name was called.

"And now the announcement you've all been dying for," the Political Alliances teacher trilled, the frills on her evening gown fluttering as she moved. "The dux of this year's cohort!"

Sweat slicked Mercury's palms. Irritated, she reached over and wiped them on Sparky's thigh.

Sparky pushed Mercury's hands back into her own personal space bubble and Mercury, nervous to the edge of distraction, let her.

"Will you please join me in welcoming to the stage, our wonderful dux for this year, Deviran Goodsmith!"

Mercury froze halfway to standing. "Did she just say Deviran?" she whispered furiously to Sparky.

Sparky hauled her forcibly back down into her seat. "Yes," she hissed back. "Sit down, you're making a fool of yourself."

Mercury's spine snapped upright as she sat, and she arranged the folds of her long black skirt demurely. "No I'm not." She closed her eyes. "Deviran's going up to the stage, isn't he?" Even at a whisper, the misery in her voice was clear, but this time, she didn't care.

Sparky reached over and squeezed her hand.

Mercury squeezed back, lacing her fingers back through Sparky's, and held tight as all her plans and dreams vanished in front of her.

A stone had landed in her chest. That must be it. Some strange sort of magic that made her chest contract and sink, and made the world distort for just a moment, long enough to trick her into thinking Deviran had beaten her so that someone could jump in front of her and yell SURPRISE!

Any moment now.

Any moment.

She refused to open her eyes and watch Deviran parading across the stupid stage like some stupid stupid-person, receiving his stupid medal and stupid symbolic crest pin.

It was that last exam question. She'd known Deviran would pull out his ridiculous 'Evil Overlords are merely figureheads, the Business Guild is where the power really lies' rant that everyone had heard a million times back when he was younger and angrier, and she'd tried to counter it, she really had.

She'd argued for the importance of the Overlording position, for the power of having a symbolic figure to unite the population in their hatred, for having a person able to make all the difficult, necessary decisions the Council was too weak and spineless to make... But it hadn't been enough.

Everything she'd worked for, everything she'd set out to prove—and it wasn't enough.

There were words, there were names, and then forever later, once she'd died twice already, Sparky elbowed her in the ribs. "Come on," Sparky muttered. "We're up next."

And sure enough, there was a shuffling of presenters as the last of the Powers Behind The Throne graduates departed the stage, and the next speaker announced in threatening, funereal tones, "The Overlording cohort."

Mercury blinked furiously and followed Sparky to the end of the line at the right side of the stage. The other candidates proceeded one at a time across the stage, two girls and then stupid Deviran, and then a handful more and then Sparky, and then the speaker was calling her name.

Hands fisted, Mercury tossed her head high, climbed the four steps, and marched across the stage. She wouldn't look at them, the stupid faculty who'd denied her the city she rightfully deserved, and she wouldn't look the other way either, at the classmates and crowd undoubtedly sniggering at her failure.

She shook hands with the presenter, and while he pinned the tiny crossed-swords badge on her collar, her eyes betrayed her and slid toward the audience. Her stomach flipped as she saw the crowd of parents and friends behind the rows of students, all the way to the back of the hall, twenty rows at least, illuminated by the late afternoon light streaming in through the ceiling-high windows to the right. Everyone had someone here to watch them graduate. Everyone except Weird Al—and her.

The presenter finished with her pin, muttered something to her, and offered his hand again. Mercury coldly ignored it and strode from the stage. It didn't matter. None of it mattered. Tumul Tuos was her city anyway, and no one could change that. She'd think of something. She'd take a day or two out, make some plans...

And she could always hope that Deviran would choose some other Overlording territory. He'd be stupid to, but then again, he was stupid, so. Mercury could hope.

All at once, mid-way down the steps off the stage, Mercury came to rigid attention, scanning the room.

Somewhere out there in the crowd, an exchange of power had just taken place, and it felt... unusual.

But the final few students were backing up behind her and muttering, so Mercury headed back toward her seat, craning her head all the while and searching for some sign of whatever it was that had just discharged a dizzyingly quiet amount of power into the room.

She sat, and Sparky leaned over. "Okay?"

"Mm," said Mercury. "Did you feel…" She accidentally caught the eye of the student behind her and twisted back to face the front.

"Feel what?"

Mercury turned it over in her mind. It had felt like a large shot of power discharged very quietly—but perhaps it hadn't been. Perhaps it had only been a small discharge after all, something most people wouldn't have noticed.

But still, something about it had tugged on her. It very nearly felt like something she'd felt before, only she *knew* she'd never sensed that kind of discharge. She shook her head. "Never mind. Don't worry."

Sparky sighed and straightened. "It's fine, Mercury," she said, drily exasperated. "I know you didn't win, but I promise, you'll live through it."

Mercury waved a hand for silence.

The power had just discharged again, and it had come from somewhere in the back corner, far away from the windows and light.

Impatiently, Mercury waited for the formalities to conclude. The crowd stood while the quartet played the exit march, and the stage party left, Mercury tapping her foot all the while.

The moment the last notes of the march died away, Mercury turned and headed to the back corner, weaving in and out of the students and parents who had seemed to explode slowly but inexorably out from the neat rows of seating, ignoring Sparky's calls behind her. Power, something that tugged in a way that was strange and familiar, all at once. She pushed her way through a family posing for pictures—and halted.

In the shadows of the back corner, Deviran stood with his family, with his stupid, smug little smile, looking as tall and dark and stupidly alluring as ever. Prat.

His mother, short but sleek, and his father— tall, and utterly terrifying in a way not at all diminished by his gleaming smile—gushed over him, patting his back and hugging him tight. Within moments the Principal was there, glibly shaking hands and congratulating them on the success of their son. Something flickered across his consciousness, and also Deviran's father's—some moment of recognition in response to what they were saying. But Mercury brushed it aside just as the mother brushed melodramatic tears from her cheeks and handed Deviran a silver-wrapped package about as long as her hand but half the width.

That. That was the source of the strange, magical feeling. Mercury watched hawk-eyed as Deviran unwrapped the gift. A glimpse of gold set her pulse racing—What was it? What did it do? Could she steal it?—and then the paper fell away to the floor, and Deviran stood staring wordlessly at the object in his hands, and Mercury did too.

Wide-eyed, Deviran raised his gaze to his parents, and even from where she stood Mercury could hear the reverence in his voice as he thanked them.

But Mercury had eyes only for the object. No wonder she'd felt it discharge, and no wonder it had felt both strange and familiar. In Deviran's hands lay a glorious, sunshine-gold key, large and strong—and with a handle in the shape of a stylised fish, long, flowing fins curving to make the grip.

A Key. They'd given him a Key. And not just any Key, but *the* Key, *her* Key, the Artefact of Power belonging to *her* city.

A wordless noise of wanting rose in Mercury's throat. Who cared about being dux? She needed that Key.

Keep reading! Head to
https://www.amylaurens.com/books/
kaditeos/castle/
to buy your copy now!